Chee Chee's A

Book 2

CHEE CHEE'S
BIG PLAN

By Carol Ottley-Mitchell

Illustrated By Ann-Cathrine Loo

Chee Chee's Big Plan
Text © 2012 by Carol Mitchell
Cover and Interior Artwork © 2012 by Ann-Cathrine Loo

Based on the character of Chee Chee created by Carol Mitchell and illustrated by Ann-Cathrine Loo

CaribbeanReads Publishing, Washington DC, 20006
First Edition
All rights reserved.
Printed in the USA
ISBN: 978-0-9832978-57
www.CarolMitchellBooks.com

Chee Chee is a vervet monkey who lives on the beautiful island of St. Kitts.

He lives with his seven sisters and brothers. The youngest one is growing up but still hangs on under his mother's tummy sometimes.

One day, quite by accident, Chee Chee and his younger brother Jon Jon discovered a wonderful abandoned garden full of fruit trees of every kind. They had only been to the garden one time and Chee Chee was determined to return.

He imagined he and his brothers swinging through the fruit trees, eating whatever they liked. No one lived in the house with the garden so the monkeys would be able to eat and play without being disturbed.

If only they could get inside.

The monkeys could not just scamper over the wall into the garden and eat until their tummies were full.

No, the house was surrounded by danger.

There was something or someone on every side of the house to keep the monkeys away.

Three Rottweilers lived in the house **on the left**; very fierce dogs who spent most of their time curled up in the shade of the front steps of their house.

If the monkeys got near their garden, the dogs would jump to their feet and bark with a deep bark that made even a brave monkey like Chee Chee run for cover.

The house **on the right** was even worse.

Not only did a fierce dog live there, but there was an elderly
man who was always at home.

4

He didn't like it when Chee Chee and his brothers ate the fruit from his trees. He couldn't move very quickly but he would stand near his dog and shake his long thick walking stick to scare the monkeys away.

Shura, the dog in the house **behind** the monkey's paradise, was quite calm. She liked people, but she did not like monkeys and would snarl and snap if they came near.

Chee Chee had made it past Shura once before and that was when he had discovered the abandoned garden. He had not been able to get past her since.

The monkeys would have loved to enter their garden through the **front** gate, but, the road in the front of the house was busy with traffic all day.

Chee Chee's older brother Maw thought they could get past the cars, but as brave as Chee Chee was and as delicious as the fruits in the garden were, the traffic was too dangerous to get past.

Chee Chee, Maw, and Jon Jon drew a picture of the problem.

The monkeys drew a square for each house.

The box in the middle was their garden and Chee Chee marked it with a large X.

He used stones for the dogs and people in the other houses. He moved the stones into one position then another.

"There must be a way in," he said at last.

"Let me go," Jon Jon pleaded, *"I can get by, I know it. Anyway, it's my turn. You spent hours in the garden last time."*

Chee Chee remembered the wonderful time he had spent collecting fruit in the garden.

"Well," Chee Chee said. "Every lunchtime Shura sleeps soundly under the ginger lilies. If she stays fast asleep **and** the three Rottweilers are also asleep, we can run along the wall of Shura's house and jump into our garden."

"But if any of them awake," Chee Chee continued, "it's BIG trouble. You can hide in Shura's garden, but it's a long jump from the trees in her garden to the wall of our garden."

"I made it the last time but that was because I was terrified!" Chee Chee added.

"*I can do it,*" Jon Jon said. "*I'm the fastest monkey ever!*"

And to prove it, he sped to the end of the road and back.

"*I don't know,*" Chee Chee said, "*it's a long jump.*"

"*Piece of cake,*" Jon Jon said. "*I'm the long-jump champion in my class.*"

And he showed Chee Chee once more, running and then taking a leap in front of his brother.

"*You won't have a running start up in the tree,*" *said* Chee Chee.

But Jon Jon insisted and eventually Chee Chee gave in.

"OK. We'll wait until Shura is asleep on this side of the house and I will stand guard here."

He drew an 'X' in the ground in front of Shura's house to show where he would hide.

"If she wakes up, I'll call out to you and you will have to run. We can't see the Rottweilers so we just have to hope that they are also asleep."

"I'm ready," said Jon Jon, "they'll never catch me!"

So the monkeys kept watch over the house where the dog called Shura lived.

When the sun was at its highest point, Shura felt too hot to walk around the garden. She went to her favorite place under the shade of the ginger lilies and fell asleep.

The monkeys waited until they thought she was in a deep sleep.

Then Chee Chee approached the wall slowly until he was close enough to touch it. Shura did not wake up.

Chee Chee signaled to Jon Jon and the little monkey came running.

Jon Jon climbed up on to the wall and ran along it towards the back of the house.

Half way there, he stopped. The Rottweilers were awake and they were already snarling at him.

"Don't panic," Chee Chee said softly. *"Jump into the trees in Shura's garden. She's still asleep."*

So little Jon Jon jumped into the fruit trees and made his way from one to another until he was in the tree next to the wall that separated Shura's house from their garden.

It was a plum tree with thickly intertwined leaves and branches, so he was hidden from the dogs below. He crept to the edge of the furthest branch and stopped.

"*Chee Chee,*" Jon Jon cried out. "I *don't think I can do it.*"

Shura rolled over in her sleep.

Chee Chee ran over to the other side of the front of the garden.

"*Shhhh,*" he whispered, "*you'll wake up Shura.*"

"*I can't do it, I can't*" wailed Jon Jon.

Chee Chee encouraged him. "*Of course you can, you're the long–jump champion, remember? You can do it.*"

"*I can't, I can't,*" Jon Jon said again.

Chee Chee knew that Jon Jon was terrified.

"Okay, don't fuss," he said, *"Just turn around and come back before Shura wakes up."*

But it was too late. While Chee Chee was talking to Jon Jon, Shura had woken.

She smelt Jon Jon and barked.

She ran under the plum tree searching for the monkey.

Jon Jon's body was well hidden, but his long tail hung down, just within Shura's reach. She leapt and nipped at his tail.

"*Owwwwww!*" Jon Jon cried, and he ran, jumping from tree to tree and then over the wall to where Chee Chee waited.

The two monkeys ran back home. Jon Jon's father wrapped leaves around his tail to soothe the cut from Shura's bite.

Jon Jon sat whimpering, "*I'm sorry, I'm sorry, I was so sure I could do it!*"

"*Don't worry, it's very difficult. We'll get there one day,*" Chee Chee comforted him.

"*She wouldn't have caught me if my tail had not been hanging down. That's the only reason she saw me,*" said Jon Jon.

He looked at his wounded tail sadly.

Chee Chee jumped up and shouted. *"That's it! Jon Jon, you got it, you found the answer!"*

Jon Jon looked puzzled, but he was pleased that he had helped his big brother.

Chee Chee said to Maw,

"I have a plan. Come with me."

The two older monkeys left Jon Jon nursing his tail and went back to the drawing that Chee Chee had made in the dirt. Chee Chee quickly explained his plan.

Maw thought about it and then agreed.

"Yes, if we move quickly, it just might work."

Maw thought a bit more and then he said, *"I'll go this time, I'm bigger than both you and Jon Jon and if I have to jump from the tree to the wall, I just might make it."*

The monkeys went to a plot of land where a new house was being built and found a piece of rope about two feet long in a coil on the ground.

The monkeys picked up the rope.

"We'll bring it back soon," Chee Chee said to Maw who did not like taking something that did not belong to them.

They ran back to Shura's house. Maw held the rope tightly in his arms.

Shura was still awake and alert. She started barking as soon as she heard the monkeys coming. Maw leapt bravely on to the wall with the rope in his mouth. He leapt from tree to tree until he got to the plum tree.

Shura also went to the plum tree. She ran in circles, jumping and barking because she could smell the monkey in the tree, but she couldn't see him.

Maw tied the rope to a branch and let it hang down until it was just out of Shura's reach. The rope looked and smelt like a monkey's tail.

Shura jumped at the rope, barking angrily and trying to bite it but try as she might, she could not touch it.

Shura was so busy trying to bite the rope she didn't see Maw slink into a nearby tree,

down the trunk,

across the lawn, and

over the wall into the abandoned garden.

He ate to his heart's content and gathered fruit to carry home for his family.

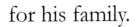

Continue the adventure with book 3:

Chee Chee's Lost Paradise

in which Chee Chee must uncover the mystery of the disappearing fruit.

Collect all five Chee Chee books or buy the Complete Collection, proceeds of which benefit the Children of the Caribbean Foundation.

Visit caribbeanreads.com or carolmitchellbooks.com

CPSIA information can be obtained
at www.ICGtesting.com
Printed in the USA
LVIC062044250620
658915LV00001B/7